About the author

Ann Jungman is the author of over one hundred books for children, specialising in mythical monsters being tamed by the modern world.

Ann was born in London and still lives there, apart from two months spent annually in Australia. Her most recent titles are **The Prince Who Thought He was a Rooster and Other Jewish Stories** (Frances Lincoln), and **Betrayal!** (Barrington Stoke) and **The Footballing Frog** (Harper Collins).

Ann is also the managing director of Barn Owl Books.

D1638939

4 3395010030984427726012

Other books by Ann Jungman

Ann Jungman

FURTHER ADVENTURES OF
Frank N. Stein
and the
GREAT GREEN GREEDY GARBAGE
MONSTER

Illustrated by Jan Smith

BARN OWL BOOKS

157 Fortis Green Road, London, N10 3LX

First published by Orchard Books, 1996 as *Monster in Trouble* and *Monster in Love*

This edition published by Barn Owl Books, 2009
157 Fortis Green Road, London, N10 3LX

Distributed by Frances Lincoln,
4 Torriano Mews, Torriano Avenue, London, NW5 2RZ

ISBN 978 19 0 301580 3

Designed and typeset by Skandesign Limited
Produced in Poland by Polskabook

www.barnowlbooks.com

CONTENTS

Trouble

Frank N. Stein smiled as he showed Steinasaurus Rex their picture in the paper.

"Read out what it says, my boy Frank," said the monster, grinning broadly.

So Frank read, "Ever since nine-year-old Frank N. Stein and his friends built the monster, Steinasaurus Rex, in a garage and he came to life, they have been best friends. Steinasaurus Rex has proved very valuable to the country as the world's biggest Rubbish Disposing Machine."

The monster giggled. "I'm in the papers a lot aren't I, my boy Frank?"

"You certainly are," agreed Frank.

Each day a huge lorry arrived to collect the monster and take him off to work. Frank would stand at the front gate and wave, then he would set off for school.

Each evening Frank would wait by the gate until the monster came home. As the monster was driven back down the road, people would lean out of their windows to welcome him back.

Steinasaurus Rex lived in a specially built shed at the bottom of the Stein's garden. He had his own television and sometimes the Steins would go and watch it with him.

Some evenings the monster would walk up the garden and sit outside the Stein's front room with his head inside the French windows. He would chat or watch something with them. But one evening Frank said to Steinasaurus Rex, "I can't play with you yet, I've got loads of homework to do."

"What's homework then?" asked the monster sulkily.

"Work that I have to do for school," Frank explained.

"Then why don't you do it at school?" complained the monster. "Who am I going to play with if you're busy doing this homework stuff?"

"I'll ring round my friends and find someone to come and keep you company," Frank told him. "You know Jason or Mark or Achmed or one of the other boys who helped to make you."

"It won't be the same. I want to be with my boy Frank after a long day at work."

"It's not that I don't want to be with you," Frank explained, "but I have to get this work done. If I don't I'll get into trouble at school."

"I see," sniffed the monster sadly. "All right – you do this homework and I'll have an early night."

"Come on – who would you like me to ring and ask to keep you company?" asked Frank desperately.

"No one. Don't bother about me, I'll be OK. Goodnight, my boy Frank."

The monster went into his hut and lay down with his back to Frank.

"Goodnight monster," whispered Frank and he walked up to his house feeling miserable.

"What's up?" asked his mother.

"My monster is upset because I've got to do my homework and I can't spend the evening with him."

"Oh dear," said Mrs Stein. "I've been worried that something like this would happen. Still, you must keep up with your school work. We have to give that priority."

"I offered to phone Jason or one of the others but my monster only wants me."

"We've got to sort this out," declared Mrs Stein. "You've got to be able to do your school work. We'll have to do something without hurting his feelings."

One day shortly afterwards, Frank was sitting in the garden trying to do his homework. The monster sat next to him doing his best not to distract Frank.

Eventually the monster asked, "What's in that book that's so good, my boy Frank?"

"It's a story and I've got to read it tonight for my homework."

"Read it to me then, my boy Frank."

So Frank sat and read the story to the monster. The monster listened in total silence, his eyes open wide. When Frank got to the end the monster looked up.

"Don't stop reading, Frank, I was really enjoying that."

"But it's the end of the story, Monster."

"Oh, can't I hear it again then?"

"There are other stories you know."

"Other stories. Lots of other stories?"

"Yes," replied Frank.

"And they're all in books?"

"Ummm,"

"That's wonderful, Frank. Can I learn to read so I can read the stories myself."

Frank stared at his monster. It had never even crossed his mind that the monster would like to be educated.

"Yes, I don't see why you shouldn't learn to read. I'll talk to my teacher about it."

Frank's teacher loved the idea of teaching the monster to read and came every day after school and sat in the garden teaching him.

The children in Frank's class took it in turns to help the monster and soon he began to read all the time.

So every day the monster went off to eat rubbish and every evening he practised his reading. He seemed totally happy. That is until one day Frank and the monster walked down the garden path and were greeted with a street blocked by dust-carts, and angry bin men shouting and waving banners.

"Down with Steinasaurus Rex!" shouted the bin men.

The monster looked around sadly and a tear ran down his face.

"They don't like me, Frank. What did I do to make them angry?"

"You're threatening our jobs, that's what," cried an angry man. "Soon they'll be sending you up and down the streets eating all the rubbish straight out of the dustbins and then none of us will have a job. We've got families to feed you know."

"I don't understand, Frank," said the monster getting more and more miserable.

Mr and Mrs Stein joined Frank and the monster by the gate.

"Take Steinasaurus back to his shed," said Mr Stein firmly. "Now what is going on here?"

"We've blocked both ends of the street and we're not letting that monster leave until we get an agreement that he doesn't do anything to interfere with our jobs," declared one of the bin men. "And he won't get a morsel of rubbish until we get that in writing from him."

More Trouble

The next morning the crowd was there again. This time it was much bigger.

Frank and his monster sat in the garden and wondered what to do next. The monster had tears running down his face.

"I don't understand," he said miserably. "I thought the people wanted me to eat their rubbish. I thought it was a good thing that I was doing, I don't understand."

"Well I'm not absolutely clear about what is going on either," replied Frank frowning. "You stay here and I'll go and see if I can find someone to talk sense to."

So Frank went out into the street and confronted the angry people waving their banners in front of the gate. "Can I talk to the person in charge?" he asked.

"We don't want to talk to you," said a big

man. "We want to talk to Steinasaurus Rex."

"Yes," said Frank, "and I'm sure he'll be happy to talk to you but neither of us understands what's happening. My poor monster hasn't been around very long and he doesn't know what he's doing wrong."

"I'll tell you what he's doing wrong, mate. That monster of yours might eat his way through our jobs."

"I see," replied Frank. "No, actually I don't see – I mean, dear Steinasaurus Rex only goes to tips and eats all the rubbish that's there. How can that harm your jobs? You collect the rubbish in our dustbins and take it to the tips. I don't understand what our monster has got to do with that?"

"That's the way it is at the moment but we've heard rumours that they're going to get Steinasaurus to eat the rubbish directly from the dustbins."

"Oh dear," sighed Frank. "That's the first we've heard of it but I can see why you're upset. Why not come through into the back garden and talk to the monster himself.

Then the man stood on the garden wall. "Friends, I am going into the back garden of this house to discuss our problem face to face with the monster."

Cheers went up and cries of, "You tell him, Dave!" and "Jobs for People not for Monsters."

So Frank and Dave went through into the back garden and Dave was introduced to the monster.

"Steinasaurus this is Dave, he represents the bin men."

"Hello," said the monster with a big grin, holding out his hand. "Pleased to meet you, Dave. Are you still angry with me?"

"Well, I don't know yet," said Dave and he explained the situation to the monster.

"But I don't want to take your jobs away," cried Steinasaurus. "All I want to do is eat rubbish. I thought that was what people wanted.

"Yes, mate, well it is. We just need to sort a few things out."

"I wish you'd hurry up," moaned the monster, rubbing his tummy. "I'm that hungry," and he reached out into the garden shed and ate the lawn mower, the rake, two spades and a hoe, and four packets of weed killer.

Dave looked at Steinasaurus in horrified amazement.

"I'll get the lads to bring him a little snack," he said and ran off.

A few minutes later a human chain was set up to get rubbish from the dust carts to Steinasaurus.

Just then Mrs Stein came out into the garden. When Frank and Dave explained what was happening she got very worried and phoned Mr Stein to come home.

"The whole street is blockaded, we've got to do something quickly."

At the moment the police turned up. "You've got to stop your people blocking the street," the policeman told Dave. "Or we'll have to start making arrests."

"The best thing would be to get the monster out of the way for a while," cried Dave. "My lads are a good bunch, they're just worried about their jobs. With Steinasaurus out of the picture for a while we might get an agreement. I'll tell my men that talks will be going on and persuade them to go home."

"Let's take up that invitation to go to Germany," cried Mrs Stein. "They've been wanting our monster to go and eat some of their rubbish. Steinasaurus will get a great welcome there."

"Brilliant idea!" said Dave.

"Germany!" exclaimed Frank. "There's a football match I wanted to go to in Stuttgart, how fantastic! All right with you Steinasaurus?"

"Anywhere, my boy Frank," mumbled the monster through the dustbin he had his head buried in. "Anywhere you are is fine by me."

So when Mr Stein got home all the plans were made. The next day Frank, his parents and Steinasaurus were all in a specially chartered plane headed for Germany.

Even More Trouble

When the Steins and Steinasaurus Rex got off the plane in Germany they were greeted by photographers, journalists and TV cameras. The monster caused a stir when he grabbed some of the cameras and ate them.

"Sorry," said Mr Stein. "He's a bit peckish I'm afraid."

Someone rushed off and soon seven dustbins, overflowing with rubbish, were driven across the tarmac. Steinasaurus ate every last bit while the remaining cameras clicked and whirred.

"That's even better," he told the journalists.

"Now that I'm not hungry you can ask me as many questions as you like."

That night on the television screens of Germany there were long interviews with the monster talking about how Frank had made him and how he was looking forward to eating a lot of German rubbish. Steinasaurus Rex enjoyed watching himself on the screen but was puzzled at the writing underneath.

"What are they there for, my boy Frank?"

"They're subtitles in German. The people here speak German not English."

"Oh," said the monster, looking a bit puzzled. "You mean not everyone speaks English."

"That's right," agreed Frank "There are hundreds and hundreds of languages in the world."

"Oh dear," sighed the monster. "But I can only speak English. Will I have to learn all those other languages Frank?"

"No," Frank told the monster soothingly. "You see lots of people speak English, it's the international language."

"I see," nodded the monster. "Good for you and me Frank eh? But maybe we should learn some of those other languages. What do you think?"

Frank agreed. They sat down and Frank read the monster a story while the monster tried to follow by putting his finger on the words as Frank said them.

The next day a lorry came to fetch Steinasaurus. The monster climbed into the lorry and drove through the streets waving to people and blowing kisses. Soon the streets were blocked and huge traffic jams built up as cars stopped to stare at the monster and wave.

When they finally did get to the rubbish dump there was big crowd waiting, all shouting and waving banners in the air.

"Oh no!" groaned Frank. "Not again."

The monster's eyes filled with tears, "Have I done something wrong, Frank? I thought they wanted me here in Germany."

Frank took the monster's big hand and squeezed it.

"Don't worry, monster, you haven't done anything wrong. You wait there and I'll try to find out what's wrong.

Frank climbed down out of the lorry. They were surrounded by demonstrators and a sea of banners.

The monster sat in the lorry and howled. "All I want to do is eat the rubbish. Why is everyone against me?"

"You've upset my monster," shouted Frank angrily. "Will someone please tell me what's going on."

"Kann jemand hier Englisch sprechen?" called a man.

"I can," said a pretty red-headed woman pushing her way towards Frank and the monster. She held out her hand to Frank. "My name's Carla. Can I help?"

"I'm confused," Frank told her. "And my poor monster is very upset. We were invited here be the German government."

"This must seem very strange. Let me explain – we're from the Green Party."

"What does that mean?" grumbled the monster. "You don't look green, you look just like everyone else."

Carla laughed. "We call ourselves Green, because we want to protect the earth, particularly green bits like grass and trees."

"Trees," nodded the monster, "I like trees. I like to rest under them in the summer. But everyone like trees."

"Yes, but huge areas of trees have to be destroyed each year just to make all the paper we need."

"Paper?" cried the monster. "Is paper made from trees?"

"Yes and that is why we don't want you to

eat paper. We know you could be very useful but if you eat absolutely everything you could do a lot of harm in the long run."

The monster began to cry loudly again.

"Steinasaurus stop it," shouted Frank. "Carla wants to talk to you."

The monster's tears were so big that everyone had to hand over their scarves so that he could mop his eyes.

"Steinasaurus, on behalf of the Greens of Germany, may I welcome you to our country," said Carla into a microphone.

There was a burst of clapping and cheering. The monster managed a little smile and a wave.

"I don't get it," he said. "You're saying you're pleased to see me but you don't want me to eat your rubbish."

"No," cried Carla. "We do want you to eat our rubbish... but not all of it."

"Oh," muttered the monster. "Now why would that be?"

"Because we think people are using up the world's resources too fast and we want some of the rubbish to be recycled."

"Rebiked?" said the monster, scratching his head in confusion. Everyone laughed which pleased the monster.

"No, recycled. Old paper can be made into new paper so we don't have to cut down trees. And glass can be turned into new bottles, and old cans into new ones."

"Paper?" said the monster brightening. "Paper – what books are made of?"

Frank and Carla nodded.

"I like books," Steinasaurus told them. "My boy Frank reads me stories from books and I'm learning to read. All right then, I won't eat paper. I'll make a pile of paper separately."

"And bottles and cans," asked Carla.

"Oh all right," groaned the monster. "Though I do really like cans. Bottles are all right but cans are absolutely yummy."

"Please Steinasaurus, we really do need to recycle the cans and bottles."

"Umm," nodded Steinasaurus. "It will make more work but it makes sense too."

"Hurray!" yelled the crowd, as they folded their banners and walked away.

By the end of the day the tip was empty and around the edge was a huge pile of paper, a pile of glass and a pile of cans.

That night Frank read Steinasaurus four stories because he had worked so hard.

"I like stories, Frank," said Steinasaurus. "Read me just one more."

But while Frank searched for a fifth story the monster fell into a much deserved sleep.

Yet More Trouble

The next morning Frank ran down to the hut that had been specially built for the monster, and found Steinasaurus Rex munching away at a big bin of rubbish.

"Look, Frank, it's from those nice Green people." He held up a big card. "I can read it all on my own. It says: 'To Steinasaurus Rex. Welcome to Germany and thank you for all your help. Carla and the Greens.'"

"Oh well done, Monster," cried Frank, beaming with pride.

"You've learned to read!"

"Could you get me more books, my boy Frank, books with stories and pictures."

"'Course," said Frank. "When we get back home, as many as you want."

Just then Mrs Stein came running towards them.

"The British Ambassador has just arrived in a big car," she told them. "She wants to talk to Steinasaurus Rex urgently."

"What's an ambassador?" asked the monster, munching his breakfast.

"She's the representative of the British Government here in Germany and it seems they think it would be better if you left Germany for a while."

The monster shook his head and looked miserable.

"But I thought I did everything right yesterday."

"You did, you did. Come and talk to the ambassador, she's waiting in the street,"

So the monster lumbered into the street, muttering to himself, "Interrupt me eating my breakfast, I don't know ..."

"Good morning, Steinasaurus Rex," said the ambassador, smiling happily. "I'm Emma Lindsay. I am thrilled to meet you."

She held out her hand.

"Have I done something bad again?" asked the monster, looking tearful.

"Oh no, nothing like that. You've been wonderful. The only thing is that the Germans need time to build all the recycling plants. They would like you to come back in six months or so."

"Oh," said the monster, looking puzzled. "So we're going home to London?"

"Well, no … We have had an urgent request from the Philippine Government. They desperately need help with their rubbish problems. They were hoping that you would be willing to go there straight away. Would you agree to do that?"

"I'm fed up," said the monster. "Nothing but trouble wherever I go. I'm well and truly fed up. I'm only trying to help."

To the Stein's horror the monster picked up the ambassador's big car. He was about to crunch it up when Emma Lindsay shouted, "Put the car down, Steinasaurus Rex. My chauffeur is in there."

The monster looked into the car, pulled out the chauffeur, patted him on the head, put him down ... and then ate the car.

"That's better," sighed the monster.

"I always feel better after a bit of breakfast. Now what was that you said? Something about the Philippines was it?"

"Yes," said the Emma Lindsay, looking sadly at half a wheel, which was all that was left of her car. "They really do need your help urgently, their rubbish tips are overflowing. We were hoping you'd be willing to go and help out."

"Oh, I'll go anywhere to help out," said the monster amiably, "just so long as my boy Frank is there and I can have some books to read."

"Excellent," smiled the ambassador. "Then that's all settled. Now perhaps you would invite me and my chauffeur to breakfast while we arrange for another car to be brought out here."

"We'd be delighted," declared Mrs Stein.

"Sorry about the car," said the monster, "but I was that hungry and cars are delicious."

"It was a new experience watching my car being eaten," said the ambassador, "and I took a great photo of you guzzling the official auto."

The ambassador and her chauffeur came to the airport to see the Steins and the monster off on the plane to the Philippines.

"Bye," they called and they waved. "Come back soon."

The Steins and the monster flew all the way to the Philippines. They slept until midday after their arrival because they were jetlagged. Just as Steinasaurus Rex was complaining about being hungry and was busy eating all the lamps and railings outside the hotel, a lorry arrived to collect them, and the monster and Frank set off. As they got near the rubbish dump the smell became terrible.

"It smells rather strong, Frank," commented the monster.

"Yuk, it smells awful," said Frank getting out his hankie and holding it to his nose. "It's because it's so hot here."

"Smells great to me," said Steinasaurus. "I can't wait to eat it."

When the lorry stopped and they got out, Frank and the monster noticed that there was a ring of people holding hands round the rubbish tip.

"What's going on Frank?" grumbled the monster. "I don't get it."

"I think they're protecting the tip," said Frank in a puzzled tone. "Like we children did when we wanted to protect you."

A man came up to them. "Mr Rex, I am Pedro and I speak for the tip dwellers. We want you to go away and not eat this rubbish because it is our livelihood."

"We don't understand," Frank told him.

"Many of us are very poor here and we make our living by finding things on the rubbish dumps and selling them. Whole families live like this."

"Live on a dump!" shouted the monster.

"That's terrible, dumps are all right for monsters but not for people."

"Yes, agreed Pedro, "But there are no jobs. At least this way we feed our children."

"But this dump smells," complained the monster. "It can't be good for your families to live here."

"This is true," said Pedro sadly.

"I've got an idea," cried Frank. "Why don't we leave you to take whatever you want from the tip and my monster will only eat what you don't want."

"Oh yes," smiled Pedro.

"I've got an even better idea," cried Steinasaurus. "I'll give you the money I get for

clearing up the rubbish tips – I don't need money. Then you can build homes and schools, far away from the tips."

"Oh that sounds wonderful. You are a brilliant monster. I need to tell my people."

Steinasaurus lifted Pedro up. After Pedro had kissed the monster on both cheeks he told the tip dwellers of the deal the monster was offering. The crowd surrounding the tip came and stood round Steinasaurus and clapped and cheered.

So Steinasaurus cleared up all the rubbish tips in the Philippines and at each tip he gave all his earnings to the tip dwellers.

After a week or two there were no more tips left for the monster to eat.

"Can we go home now, Frank?" asked the monster anxiously. "I'm homesick, I want to go back to my hut in your garden."

"I want to go home too," Frank told him "and so do Mum and Dad. I think we should leave as soon as possible."

The next day as the Steins and Steinasaurus walked across the tarmac at Manila airport they saw their plane was surrounded by people waving banners.

They got on to the plane garlanded with flowers and everyone sang and waved. Tears ran down the monster's face.

"I really helped them, didn't I Frank?"

"Yes, Steinasaurus, you certainly did."

No More Trouble

The Steins sat in the hold of the plane that had been sent for them and looked at each other.

"So much has happened," commented Mr Stein. "I can hardly take it in."

"I know," agreed the monster. "Protests by bin workers in England."

"And Greenies up in arms in Germany," added Mrs Stein.

"And if that wasn't enough," said Frank grinning. "The tip dwellers in Manila got together to keep us out."

The monster roared with laughter. "One way or another I wasn't popular was I?"

"You were not," agreed Mrs Stein. "But you seem to have won them all round Steinasaurus Rex."

"I know", giggled the monster. "Because I never wanted to do anyone any harm. Once everyone understood that we worked it all out."

"Listen to this," said Mr Stein rusting a newspaper. "Just look at this…"

GREEN MONSTER POINTS THE WAY TO THE FUTURE

The Green Party of Germany and the German Government have come to an agreement about recycling rubbish. The agreement was reached after a crisis caused by British rubbish-eating monster, Steinasaurus Rex. Both sides said they were grateful to the monster for highlighting the issue.

"Show me," shouted Steinasaurus, grabbing the paper. "Hey look Frank, there's a picture of me eating the ambassador's car. That was a bit naughty, wasn't it?"

56

"Yes," said Mr Stein, "and it was more than a bit naughty when you ate my car. You've got to stop it."

"It's very hard," moaned the monster. "I mean, they want me to eat old cars but not new ones. How am I supposed to know?"

"It's very simple," Mr Stein told him. "When in doubt, don't eat anything!"

"What are you going to do when we get home, monster?" asked Frank.

"I'm going to read lots of books, my boy Frank. That's what I'm going to do."

"Yes," said Frank. "But I meant what are you going to do about the bin men?"

"Oh, you don't have to worry about them Frank."

"Oh," said Mr Stein. "And how is that?"

"You'll see," replied the monster. "After all my experiences I've learned a thing or two. I've worked out how to make Dave and his mates feel safe about their jobs.

They arrived in London and drove home. Along the streets they noticed overflowing dustbins and loads of black bags.

"Oh dear," sighed Mr Stein. "Look there's rubbish everywhere. They still out on strike."

"Don't worry," smiled the monster. "I'll sort it out in no time, no need to worry yourselves."

When they got back to the house there were reporters waiting for them. As the monster got out of his lorry they crowded round and a dozen cameras flashed.

"Do you have anything to say about what happened in Germany," asked one of the reporters.

"Are you glad to be home?" yelled another.

"What about the strike here?" called another. "Do you have any views on that."

"Yes, and what about the Philippines?" cried someone else.

"Let us through," said Mr Stein angrily. "We've all had a very long trip and are very tired. None of us has anything to say."

"I do," said Steinasaurus Rex firmly and he sat down on the front path. "I've got lots and lots to say."

And Steinasaurus told them all about what had happened in Germany and in the Philippines. Then he said, "And the problem here in Britain can be solved very easily too. I want to use this opportunity to say to all the bin men of this country that I am not going to take away their jobs. What I want to suggest is that they collect all the rubbish and sort it into piles, just like in Germany. Then when that is all done I will eat what is left. That pleases everyone. The rubbish gets recycled, the bin men keep their jobs, I get plenty to eat, and everyone loves me. What could be better than that?"

"Well the government might not accept that," said one journalist. "I mean it would be very expensive."

"I've thought about that," said the monster

proudly, "I've been reading about it. All the money I earn here can go to building big, modern recycling centres and if the government doesn't agree I will stop eating rubbish and eat cars instead. Now I am very tired and am going to go to sleep for a while. Thank you gentlemen, but I have nothing more to say. Good-bye."

The next morning when Frank woke up he ran down to the bottom of the garden,
"Morning, Monster," he called. "How are you feeling this morning?"

No answer. Frank opened the door and peered into the hut. No monster. Frank raced up to the house.

"Mum, Dad, our monster has gone again!" Just then Frank spotted a not one the front door:

Frank stared in amazement. "My monster can write," he said proudly. "First he learned to read and then he learned to write. Well, good for him. Good old Steinasaurus Rex."

That evening all the Steins watched the seven o'clock news on TV. Steinasaurus sat in the garden, yawning and stretching with his head through the French windows.

"I'm on the news," he told the Steins. "Just you watch and see."

And he was. There was the monster walking down streets taking dustbins from the bin men, scoffing the contents, giving them back and taking more.

"The streets of London are cleaner today than they have been for years," said the reporter. "Thanks to our wonderful British monster, Steinasaurus Rex. We understand that a new agreement is being drawn up in which the monster and the bin men will work together for a cleaner Britain. The future is looking good for British rubbish."

"Here, here," grinned the monster, and then he burped and giggled. "Oh, pardon me," he said, "but I have eaten rather a lot of rubbish today!"

The Rebiking Centre

"Just look at that!" cried Steinasaurus Rex to his friend and creator Frank N. Stein. There in front of them was a huge sign.

"It looks great, Steinasaurus," said Frank, glowing with pride. "But you know it should be recycling not rebiking."

"I call it rebiking," insisted Steinasaurus. "Monsters prefer rebiking," and he began to munch his way through pile of bricks.

Frank sighed, "Don't eat the bricks, they're for building your centre."

"But they're nice, my boy Frank."

"That's not the point," replied Frank.

"Don't you think I've chosen a good way to spend all the money I've earned eating rubbish all over the world, my boy Frank?"

"It's very good, monster," smiled his friend. "They'll be bringing paper and glass here from all over the country."

But the monster was too busy munching away at a digger truck to hear.

"That's better," he grinned. "I felt peckish."

Then he picked up a piece of scaffolding and wolfed it down. Just as Steinasaurus was about to eat the cement mixer the foreman rushed up, mopping his brow.

"Steinasaurus Rex, will you put that thing down, put it down this very second. Honestly Frank, I know this monster you made eats rubbish, but how are we supposed to get this building finished if he eats all the material and the machines."

"Sorry," mumbled the monster, "I get hungry, you see."

"I'll keep him away," interrupted Frank. "I'll see to it that he doesn't come to the site again until the building is finished."

"But I want to watch my centre being built," grumbled the monster.

"Steinasaurus Rex, if you're here the building won't be finished on time. I tell you what. Let's go home and organise the best party ever to celebrate the opening of the biggest Recycling Centre in the whole wide world."

"A party!" yelled Steinasaurus. "I would love a party. Listen everyone, you're all invited to my party. Come on, Frank, let's go, we've got big plans to make."

So the big truck that transported Steinasaurus Rex around picked them up, and they went off waving to the workmen.

That evening Frank and his monster sat in the garden outside the monster's hut and made a list of who they were going to invite to the party. It came to nearly 300 people. Frank designed an invitation.

Come and help us to celebrate the opening of the world's first and biggest Rebiking Centre. Frank.N.Stein and steinasaurus Rex invite you to the opening of the steinasaurus Rex Rebiking Centre on saturday 15th June to be followed by a wonderful ParTY at: Lot 107, The JuBilee IndustriaL Estate, South Brockton

RSVP steinasaurus Rex.

"We ought to get someone famous to open your centre," Frank told the monster.

"I don't know anyone famous," said the monster, shaking his head. "Do you?"

"Maybe one of the stars from a Frankenstein film?" suggested Frank.

"Oooh," said the monster, his eyes lighting up, "I'd love to see one of those films. Could you get one on video for me?"

So Frank and the monster went to the video shop, and Frank went in and got the movie *Frankenstein*. Back at the house Frank put it on and the monster sat in the garden with his head stuck through the French windows, tears running down his face.

"That poor monster, everyone was so mean to him that he turned into a bad monster. Not like me, eh Frank?"

"No you were always a nice monster," said Frank, holding the monster's hand and squeezing it.

"But I might have been bad, Frank. If everyone had run away and been scared."

"You were lucky," Frank told him. "You were made by children and we wouldn't be that daft."

"I like that pretty lady in the film," said the monster. "Do you think she might come and open my Rebiking Centre?"

"We could ask her," nodded Frank. "I think I read somewhere that she was very interested in green issues."

"Does that mean she would approve of my Rebiking Centre?" asked the monster.

"Probably," said Frank. "We'll write her a letter together and explain the situation, and then maybe she'll agree to come."

"We'll do it as soon as the film is over," agreed the monster, and he continued to cry over the bad treatment of the monster until the film ended.

Brides of Frankenstein

"There's a letter for me," yelled the monster, as Frank opened the gate on his way home from school. "Quick, read it to me, it may be from the lady in the film."

"I thought you were learning to read," said Frank, as he took the letter.

"Oh I am, my boy Frank, but I find people's writing a bit difficult. Read it please, please, please!"

Frank opened the envelope and read:

Dear Steinasaurus Rex and Frank N. Stein,

Thank you so much for your kind invitation to open your recycling centre (I presume the rebiking was a joke or a mistake.) I am delighted to accept. As you probably know, I am concerned about the environment and very much approve of the new centre you are planning.

Looking forward to meeting you on the fifteenth of June.

Yours

Marina Dodgson.

"She's going to come!" shouted the monster and he picked Frank up and threw him in the air.

"Put me down," yelled Frank, kicking his legs in the air and shaking his fist at Steinasaurus Rex.

"Sorry," said the monster, "I got a bit carried away."

"No you didn't, it was me who got carried away," grumbled Frank, straightening out his clothes. "Now don't do that again Steinasaurus Rex, it makes me feel seasick."

As the day for the grand opening of the Rebiking Centre approached the monster and the Steins began to feel very excited.

On the fourteenth of June, the day before the party – they drove out to the centre.

"It hardly looks like the same place," said Mrs Stein. "Those bowls of flowers make all the

difference, and the tables with umbrellas give it a lovely atmosphere."

"Yes," agreed Mr Stein. "And all the bunting and the flags. It's very colourful"

"You're right," said Frank. "And when that big sheet thing comes down revealing the name, 'The Steinasaurus Rex Rebiking Centre,' it will look very grand."

The next day, people swarmed into the centre. They were all given drinks and then waited for the official opening. On the dot of 3pm Marina Dodgson climbed on to the stage. Behind her sat the Steins, the monster, mayor and the council. As she stood up to speak lots of flashes went off.

"It's only the newspaper people taking pictures," Frank whispered to the monster, who was looking a bit alarmed.

"Having appeared in the film of Frankenstein," she began, I was a bit nervous of meeting another Frank N. Stein and his monster, but they turned out to be quite different from the originals."

Everyone laughed. "And now I have great pleasure in declaring this Recycling Centre..."

"Rebiking," yelled the monster fiercely. "Rebiking Centre! What's the matter with everyone?"

"This...um...Rebiking Centre – open," said the actress. "I would like to use this occasion to remind everyone that the earth's resources are limited and it is crucial that we recycle as much as we can. I hope that this centre, kindly donated to the nation by Steinasaurus Rex, will be much used and will be only the first of its kind."

Everyone clapped and cheered. The actress pulled the cord and there, in bright letter was: 'THE STEINASAURUS REX REBIKING CENTRE – bring your paper, glass and cans to be rebiked here'.

Steinasaurus took the microphone and ate it.

"Oh no," groaned Frank N. Stein "You were supposed to make a speech."

"I'll shout," said the monster. "I've got a big voice, I was just a bit peckish, my boy Frank, nothing to get het up about." The monster turned to address the crowd.

"Thank you all for coming to the opening of my Rebiking Centre. I hope you will all use it, particularly for paper. You see, I really like reading books and I'm very worried there might not be enough paper for all the books, so please help. There's food and drink and a band, so off you go everyone, and have good time."

Everyone did have a good time. Marina Dodgson danced with Mr Stein, and then Frank, and they agreed to teach the monster how to dance. He really enjoyed himself. The monster party didn't end until one o'clock in the morning and all the parents were having so much fun they didn't even notice the time.

After the opening of the Rebiking Centre, the monster was rather quiet. Each day he went off and ate the rubbish as usual but everyone noticed that Steinasaurus Rex wasn't quite himself. He spent a lot of time alone staring into space and moping.

"He's not eating as much as he used to," the dustmen told Frank.

"He never comes to school to learn to read any more," complained the children.

"He doesn't talk to me as much as he used to either," commented Frank sadly. "I'll try to find out what the problem is."

So Frank knocked on the door of the monster's hut and called out.

"Hello, are you home? Can I come in?"

"If you want to," came the listless reply.

"What's up?" asked Frank.

"I'm in love," replied the monster, "with Marina Dodgson."

"But she's a human," said Frank. "She's very famous and beautiful."

"I know," said the monster, tears running down his cheeks. "But there are no monsters for me to love, my boy Frank. I'll have to be lonely for ever."

"Oh dear," said Frank sympathetically, handing the monster a tea towel to dry his tears. "What can we do? Let me think."

Frank and the monster sat holding hands while Frank racked his brains. Suddenly he leapt up. "I've got it, I've got an idea."

"Oooh," cried the monster. "You gave me a fright there, my boy Frank. All right then, what's the idea?"

"When I went to the video shop to get Frankenstein out there was another video called *Brides of Frankenstein*. Come on, let's go down to the video shop."

Later that night Frank and the monster sat together in the monster's hut watching the film and eating pop corn. In the film, Frankenstein made a lady monster to be a mate for the other monster.

"That's it," cried Frank N. Stein. "We'll make you a lady monster. First thing tomorrow I'll call Mark and Achmed and Chris and Jason and we'll start building another monster."

"Girls might have a better idea about a lady

monster," grumbled Steinasaurus Rex.

"You're right," said Frank. "As soon as I get to school tomorrow I'll see if the girls want to help."

"I can't wait," giggled the monster. "A lady monster and just for me."

The Lady Monster

The next day at school Frank told everyone in his class to be at a special meeting under the big oak tree in the playground.

At break the children all raced out and sat under the big tree, sipping their drinks and munching their snacks.

"What is it, Frank?" asked Achmed. "Has

something happened to our monster?"

"Well, sort of," replied Frank. He told them all about Steinasaurus Rex being lonely and wanting a lady monster. He ended up saying, "So I had a brilliant idea, I told Steinasaurus Rex that we would build him a lady monster."

There was a stunned silence, broken only when Mark said, "But Frank, Steinasaurus Rex only came alive by chance."

"I know," agreed Frank. "But we could leave the lady monster outside until there's a thunderstorm and hope for the best."

"Sounds a bit dicey to me," grumbled Jason.

"I think you're all being really boring," announced Chris. "I can't wait to build another monster. I'm going to start tonight even if the rest of you won't."

"Good," said Frank, grinning. "And Steinasaurus was hoping that the girls would help. He thought you could make a really beautiful lady monster for him."

"Hands up which girls will help," shouted Achmed.

All the girl's hands shot up.

"Great!" cried Frank. "Steinasaurus Rex knew we could rely on you. Everyone start bringing their bits and pieces to my garden on Saturday morning, and we'll get going on the bride of Steinasaurus Rex."

Just then the bell rang and the children ran to get into line, calling out to Frank, "Don't worry, Frank, we'll build a super-duper lady monster. Tell Steinasaurus that his problems are over!

On Saturday morning every member of Frank's class came up with something – and old fridge, tyres, boxes of every size and shape, old dresses, bits of lace, four hats, loads of old jewellery and much more besides.

"Put everything in the middle of the lawn," ordered Frank. "And then we can decide what we need."

Soon there was a huge pile of rubbish in the Stein's back garden. Mr Stein looked out of the window and groaned, "I don't believe it," he said and raced downstairs.

"What is going on Frank? What on earth is all this rubbish doing on my lawn?"

"We're going to build a lady monster for Steinasaurus Rex, Dad. My poor monster is sad and lonely and we want to help him."

"Oh no!" sighed Mr Stein. "Look, Frank, I'm very fond of dear old Steinasaurus Rex but I don't think we could cope with another monster around the place. There isn't room. This is a very average kind of house and garden, definitely not big enough for two monsters."

The children stood round Mr Stein looking miserable.

"But Dad," Frank said, "if Steinasaurus Rex had a wife he could go and live somewhere else. He wouldn't need us so much. He could live nearby and we could all still be friends but he'd be more independent."

"True," agreed Mr Stein. "Yes, you're quite right, Frank. All right kids, go on and make your monster. And good luck!"

So the children set to work building the monster. Steinasaurus Rex watched from his window and called encouragement and suggestions.

After a few hours the new monster began to look rather good. The girls collected some wood shavings and stuck them onto the saucepan that had been used as a head. It looked as though the monster had long blond ringlets. They then gave the monster eyes of blue beads with sequins all round them. The bright red mouth was made of red cloth and then the monster was given bright-pink cheeks.

"She looks so beautiful and healthy," sighed Steinasaurus Rex.

"We haven't finished yet," cried the children. "Just you wait and see how gorgeous we're going to make her."

All day the monster was worked on and improved. By the end of the day she lay on the lawn, wearing a long green skirt that Mrs Stein had run up, and orange top with brown sleeves that the children had pinned on her, four necklaces, earrings, a big straw hat from Marina Dodgson and a pair of red shoes made from painted shoe boxes.

"What do you think, Steinasaurus Rex?" asked the children eagerly.

"She's wonderful," said the monster, dreamily. "Just the kind of wife I want."

"Thank you everyone," cried Frank. "I think we've done a fantastic job. Mum says there's sausage rolls and a big cake for tea."

The children cheered.

"All we have to do," continued Frank, "is wait for a thunderstorm and the lightning that will bring my second monster to life."

Two weeks later the skies grew dark and overcast. It began to rain, and thunder. All the children rushed over to Frank's house and stood with their noses pressed against the French windows to see what would happen. Frank and Steinasaurus Rex sat in his hut, eagerly looking out of the window. It rained and rained, the lightning flashed through the sky and a tree nearby was hit and crashed to the ground. But the lady monster just got wetter and wetter, never showing even a flicker of life.

As the sun came out, the children filed into the garden and stood by the sodden monster, tears running down their faces.

Steinasaurus Rex banged his fists on the ground and wailed. "It didn't work, your silly old brilliant plan didn't work. My beautiful wife looks horrible. It's all your fault, Frank."

"Don't give up Steinasaurus Rex," said Frank. "We'll just have to find another way of bringing her to life."

"We'll patch her up," cried the children.

"You'll see, we'll make her a good as new in two days."

"We'll put her in the garage so she won't get wet again." added Achmed.

"Yes," agreed the other, "and we'll make her even better than new. Just you wait and see, Steinasaurus Rex."

A Broken Heart

After the storm, Steinasaurus Rex shut himself in his hut and wouldn't talk to anyone, not even Frank. The children worked hard to get the lady monster back to her former glory. In two days she was propped against the back wall of the garage, looking better than she had before.

"Come on, Steinasaurus Rex," said Frank, holding out his hand. "Come and see your lady friend. She 's looking great!"

The monster let himself to be led to the garage, where all the children were waiting expectantly. Jason and Lucy flung open the doors of the garage, grinning broadly.

Steinasaurus Rex looked at the lifeless monster and shook his head and said, "I'm very sad, my boy Frank, very sad indeed."

He walked back to his hut, hunching his shoulders and shaking his head.

As the days passed the monster stopped eating. Everyone was very worried. The dustmen came round with a whole dustbin full of banana skins.

"They're his favourite," they told the Steins. "Just put them outside his door and he won't be able to resist the smell."

But the next morning the banana skins were still there.

After a while tips began to fill up again, and no one knew what to do.

"Why don't we phone Marina Dodgson?" suggested Mrs Stein. "Our monster liked her, maybe she can help."

The next day the film star turned up with a bunch of roses. Steinasaurus Rex livened up a bit when he saw her and ate the roses.

"Everyone is so worried about you, Steinasaurus, what can we do to make you feel better?"

"Bring my beautiful lady to life," begged the monster.

"Well, maybe next time there's a really good

thunderstorm the lightning will strike and wake her up."

"No," groaned the monster, shaking his big head. "It won't happen. I love her so much but she'll never come alive, never, never!"

"Don't be so sure about that," said Marina Dodgson. "I've just had an idea."

"What idea?" asked the monster eagerly. "Go on, tell me. I really want to know."

'I've got to talk to Frank and his parents first and some other people. Then I'll let you know what I'm planning."

After that the monster cheered up enough to eat seventy-five rotten banana skins.

Marina Dodgson went to speak with the Steins.

"He doesn't believe that the lady monster will ever come to life. He says that he loves her very much and that's why he can't eat."

"He may be right about her never coming to life," said Mr Stein gloomily.

"After all it was a freak that Steinasaurus was hit by lightning, we can't really expect it to happen again."

"I agree," sighed Mrs Stein. "The chances of it happening twice must be a million to one."

"I feel so guilty," groaned Frank. "I should never have got his hopes up."

"It's not your fault, Frank," said Marina Dodgson soothingly.

"It is, it is! I should never have let the boys at school persuade me to make a monster, even though my name is Frank N. Stein. I should have said no! Now poor old Steinasaurus Rex is alive and he is very unhappy and I can't help him."

"I think you are all giving up too easily," declared Marina Dodgson.

"Well if you've got a suggestion, we'd like to hear it," said Mr Stein.

"Well here it is," said the actress. "Why did

Dr Victor Frankenstein want to make a monster in the film."

"Because he was a scientist," cried Frank.

"Exactly! I think the time has come for us to ask the scientists for their help."

"Of course!" yelled Frank. "That's it. Marina you are a genius!" and he gave her a big hug. "Scientists may be able to give her an electric charge to bring her alive."

"It's all well and good saying 'Get scientists to help'," said Mr Stein. "But which scientists? And how do we contact them? And how do we pay them."

"That's shouldn't be a problem," cried Mrs Stein. "I mean governments all over the world are worried because Steinasaurus isn't eating all the rubbish. They'll pay anything to get him back to work."

"Oh yes!" said Frank. "We can contact those government scientists who tested Steinasaurus when he first came to life. Now why didn't I think of that?"

"I think I've still got their number," said Mr

Stein, looking through his address book. "Yes, here is it, let's call them now, not a moment to lose."

The scientists were very keen to help.

"We read about it in the papers," said the chief scientist. "We're very sympathetic to poor old Steinasaurus. Of course we'll do whatever we can. It'll be a new challenge to all of us. We'll be around first thing tomorrow morning."

"Do you think they'll be able to do anything, Dad?" asked Frank.

"I don't know, Frank, but I certainly hope so. Because if they can't I don't know what we're going to do with your poor, sad monster!"

The Wonders of Science

On the dot of nine the government scientists arrived as promised. Frank was given some time off school so that he could explain to the scientists exactly what had happened.

"We made this monster out of bits and pieces, just like we made Steinasaurus Rex. But this time she won't come alive. Even the lightning didn't do it."

The scientists put on their white coats and walked round the monster, making notes and taking photographs, and asking exactly what had been used to make her.

"I think we should take her apart and find out exactly what materials are in there. Maybe we can add electrodes and some materials which will conduct electricity."

"Steinasaurus Rex mustn't see you do that," said Frank quickly. "He's upset enough as it is."

"Why don't you and I go and see him," suggested the chief scientist. "I got on with him extremely well when we last met. I'll try to make him see that all is well."

So Frank and the scientist went over to the monster's hut and found him lying on the floor staring at the ceiling. The scientist shook Steinasaurus by the hand and then told him they were going to do everything they could to bring his lady to life.

Steinasaurus nodded and said, "Thank you," in a tired voice.

"I brought you some sawdust and a few

stethoscopes," said the chief scientist. "They were your particular favourites during your stay with us, if I remember rightly."

"Yes," agreed the monster. "I did like them once. Just leave them, please. I may try and eat a little later on."

"I could boil them up and make some sawdust and stethoscope soup," suggested Frank. "You like soup."

"No," sighed the monster. "Don't bother, my boy Frank."

"I've brought you some tapes, Steinasaurus – love songs. I thought you might like to listen to them."

The monster brightened up a little.

"Love songs, Frank. Are they sad ones? Where everyone gets a broken heart?"

"Oh yes," Frank told him. "They're all very sad. Shall I play them?"

Frank put on the tapes and, as they left, tears ran down the monster's big cheeks.

The scientist and Frank went back into the garage. The lady monster lay on the floor in dozens of pieces.

"Please be quick," said Frank, "This would really upset Steinasaurus."

The scientists worked in pairs noting quickly what the lady monster was made of and then putting the pieces back. Soon she was a good as new.

"We've put lots of wires and batteries and fuses in her," they told Frank. "Now we're going to put a big electrical charge through her."

Some of the scientists were on ladders attaching things to the monster's head, other were putting wore around her feet.

"The charge is about the same as a direct hit by lightning," the scientists told Frank. "Fingers crossed, here we go."

The chief scientist pressed three switches. The monster shook for a minute or two and then slumped back as before.

"It didn't work," said Frank sadly.

"There was always only a very small chance that it would," said the chief scientist sadly. "We'll give it another try but don't get your hopes up too much."

They tried once more with exactly the same result.

"What a good thing Steinasaurus Rex didn't know what was going on in here." commented the chief scientist.

At that moment there was a terrible roar and Steinasaurus Rex reached into the garage and grabbed two of the scientists. He held them in his huge hands and glared at them.

"What have you been doing to my girlfriend? Have you been hurting her?"

"No, honestly!" squeaked the terrified scientists. "We were trying to bring her to life for you."

"Steinasaurus," shouted Frank in a stern voice. "Put those two nice people down this very minute, they have only been trying to help. No one has hurt your lady monster I promise you."

Steinasaurus Rex looked at Frank and then at the scientists and then back to his lady love.

"Come on, Steinasaurus, put them down or I won't be your friend any more."

The monster put the scientists down very gently.

"Now apologise," insisted Frank. "We've all been working very hard to help you."

"Sorry my boy Frank. Sorry scientists," mumbled the monster, and he stumbled back to his hut.

"Oh dear, he is in a bad way, poor chap," said the chief scientist. "I just wish there was something the world of science could do to help."

"We'll all work on it back at the lab," they promised, "but the chances of a breakthrough are very small."

After that the monster stopped eating all together and rubbish began to be a problem again all over the world.

Then one day Marina Dodgson arrived and announced, "I've got an idea."

"Alright," sighed Frank. "Let's hear it."

"I think the first thing we should do is get the lady monster out of the garage and put her on the lawn outside Steinasaurus' hut."

"Last time she just got drenched."

"I know, but today it's lovely and sunny," Marina Dodgson pointed out, "not a cloud in the sky."

"OK, so we get her out and then what?" demanded Frank.

"Then all the people who love Steinasaurus Rex make circles round the garden and we close our eyes and hold hands and hope and hope, as hard as we can, that she comes to life."

"That's the daftest thing I ever heard," scoffed Frank.

"We could try it at least," snapped the actress. "It couldn't do any harm."

"I suppose not," muttered Frank. "But you go and tell everyone what you want them to do. I would feel like a real idiot asking people to, well, just hope."

But to Frank's surprise, everyone was very willing to help.

So at twelve o'clock on Saturday four huge circles were formed round the Stein's house. Everyone who knew Steinasaurus Rex was there. On radio and television all over the world the call had gone out for people to close their eyes at the same time and join the 'Hope-In'. In some countries people had to wake up in the middle of the night to take part.

"This is silly," grumbled Frank, as he went over to Steinasaurus' hut to explain what was going on.

"Monster, all over the world people are closing their eyes and hoping for your lady monster to come alive They are about 2,000 people gathered outside here alone, just for that purpose."

"We're calling it a 'Hope-In'," Marina Dodgson explained. "We've asked everyone who likes you and everyone who cares about the environment to come and join in. Millions of people will be hoping that yours story has a happy ending."

"When does it start, my boy Frank?"

"In one minute," Frank told him.

Steinasaurus grabbed one of Frank's hands and one of Marina Dodgson's and they all closed their eyes tight. Then they heard the church clock strike twelve. Then there was a long silence.

Suddenly a big booming voice rang out "Steinasaurus Rex, after all the fuss you've been making where are you?"

Hardly daring to hope, they all opened their

eyes. There, standing with her hands on her hips, stood the lady monster.

"She's alive! We all hoped her to life. Oh thank you everyone," yelled Steinasaurus Rex. "My true love is alive," and he ran across the lawn and hugged the lady monster.

Everyone cheered and cheered.

Steinasaurus jumped up and down and then shouted, "I'm starving."

"Me too!" declared the lady monster.

Then before anyone could stop them, they

started to eat the tiles off the house.

"Stop!" yelled Frank.

Of course neither monster took any notice. Within minutes the Stein's house was stripped bare. The crowd gathered for the 'Hope-In" watched in amazement as the monsters munched contentedly.

"Frank," said Mr Stein. "We are going to change your name by deed poll. We are going to drop the Norman and then I forbid you to build any more monsters."

"Don't worry, Dad," sighed Frank. "I don't want to. Two are more than enough and I'll be very glad not to be Frank N. Stein any more!"